DON'T FEAR THE DOCTOR

by Michael Scotto
illustrated by The Ink Circle

WELCOME TO MIDLANDIA

OUR STORY BEGINS

Midlandia University

Community Center

Animal Land

Town Square

HERE

Playland Park

Bike Factory

Harvest Farms

KNUTE O. BOBO
The Coach

STARRING

DOC FIXIT
WANNADOGOOD
The DOCTOR

Coach was known as the
toughest athlete in Midlandia.
At Playland, he watched over all
of the games and made sure people
played safely. But sometimes,
even coaches get hurt.

Once, while refereeing a kickball game,
Coach looked away just as Chief Tatupu
launched the kickball with a mighty swing of
his leg. "**Look out, Coach!**" Chief shouted.

Coach turned back just in time to see the bright
red kickball soaring right for his nose! He jumped out
of the way at the last moment, landing with a crash.

"**Ouch...**" Coach muttered.
"Oh, my," Chief said as he ran over.
"**I am sorry!** I did not mean to send
you tumbling!"

"It's all right.
I live to tumble!"
Coach exclaimed.
"I just bumped my
ankle a little bit."

Chief helped Coach sit up, and then saw his ankle. "You have bumped it more than a little bit," Chief said. "Your ankle is as red and puffy as the kickball! **You had better go see Doc Fixit.**"

Coach did not respond. "I know your ankle must hurt," Chief said. "If you go to Doc Fixit, she could give you medicine to help with the swelling, or maybe give you a shot!"

"**A shot?!**" Coach cried. Then he grumbled, so no one would notice how worried he was.

But when Coach tried to walk away, he just stumbled. "**Oww-ie!**" he exclaimed.

"**That is it**," Chief said. "I am taking you to Doc Fixit, and there is nothing you can do about it."

Chief carried Coach toward the Town Square on his back. "You are not setting a very good example," Chief said. "You should not be so **stubborn.**"

As the two neared the Town Square,
Coach made his move and jumped off Chief's back.
"I don't want to go to the doctor!" he declared.

"**Why are you scared?**" Chief asked. "You are the toughest athlete in Midlandia!"

"Even tough athletes can be scared," Coach said.

"I know," Chief said, "but there is no reason to be scared of the doctor."

"Do you know what it's like at the doctor's office?!" Coach hissed.

and they poke at you...and those needles they have!"
Coach shuddered. **"I don't like needles."**

"Have you ever been to the doctor?" Chief asked. "I have a check-up twice every year. Doc Fixit is a **nice** woman and a **good** doctor."

"Yeah, sure," Coach said. "That's what everybody says."

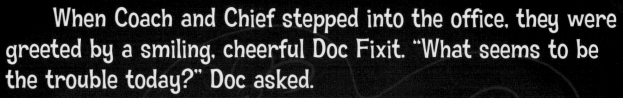

When Coach and Chief stepped into the office, they were greeted by a smiling, cheerful Doc Fixit. "What seems to be the trouble today?" Doc asked.

"I'm fine," Coach said.

"He means," Chief said, "that he fell and hurt his ankle. Can you take a look?"

"First," Doc said, "let's make sure you didn't hurt your head when you fell. I'm going to use this **little** light to check your eyes, okay?"

"That little thing?" Coach asked. **"Sure, that doesn't seem so bad."**

Doc shined the little light near Coach's eyes. **"Your eyes are fine,"** she said, "but your ears! My goodness, you need to clean them out, Coach!"

"Now let's test your reflexes to make sure you didn't hurt any other part of your leg." Doc took out a small rubber mallet. "I'm going to tap your knee with this."

The first part didn't hurt at all, so Coach said, "Okay...just not too hard." Doc tapped Coach's knee, and his leg bounced up. **"Wow!"** Coach said. **"Do that again!"**

"Now, Coach," Doc said with a smile, "I'm going to touch your ankle very lightly, and you tell me where it hurts. **Is that okay?**"

"Yeah, I guess," Coach told her.

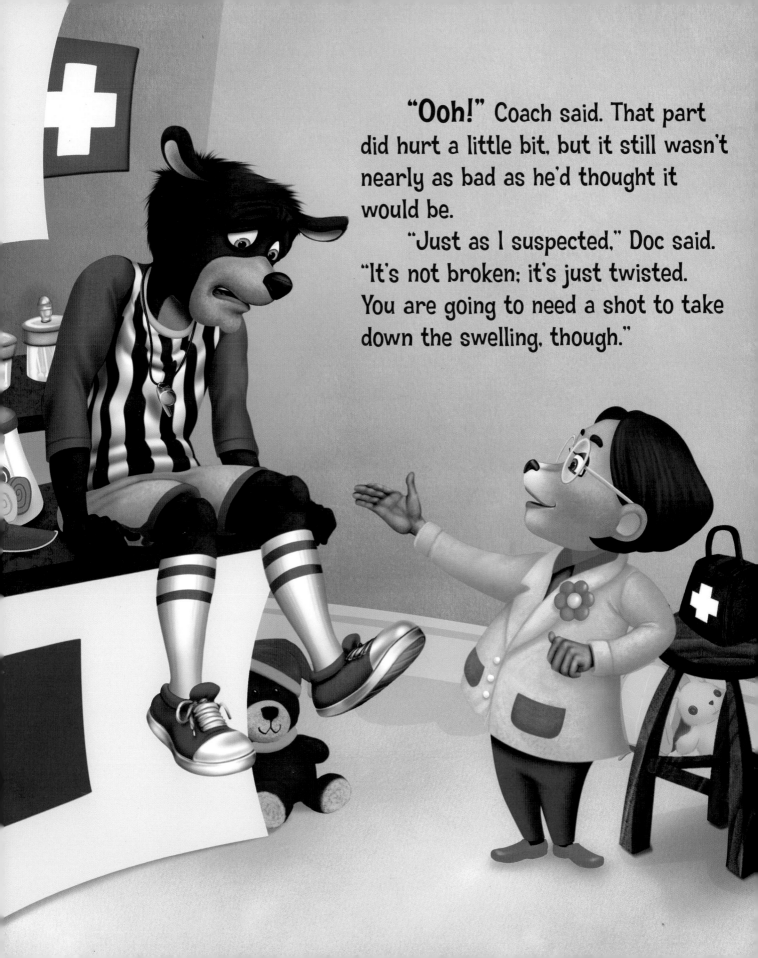

"Ooh!" Coach said. That part did hurt a little bit, but it still wasn't nearly as bad as he'd thought it would be.

"Just as I suspected," Doc said. "It's not broken; it's just twisted. You are going to need a shot to take down the swelling, though."

"**A shot!**" Coach shrieked. "Oh, no, I'm done for!"

"It's really not so bad," Doc said. "It's just a little...what's that over there?" Doc pointed to the other side of the room. While Coach looked away, she quickly gave him his shot.

Coach felt a little poke, and he looked back to Doc. "What was that little poke?" he asked.

Doc held up her needle. **"Congratulations, Coach,"** she said, "you've just had your first shot."

"You mean you did it already?" Coach cried.

The swelling started to go down right away. Coach looked at Chief. "I can't believe it!" Coach said. "I barely felt it."

"Keep off that ankle for a couple of days," Doc said, "and you'll be better in no time."

Chief helped Coach down the road toward his house. "All this time I've been scared of the doctor, and there was no reason at all!" Coach said.

"I am glad you can see that doctors are here **to help you, not scare you,**" Chief said.

A few days later, Coach was back in action on the field. From then on, he always made sure that if someone got hurt at Playland, they went to the right place: **straight to the doctor.**

DISCUSSION QUESTIONS

Can you think of a time when you were afraid of something, but overcame your fears? What did you learn?

Have you ever been hurt or sick? How did a doctor help?